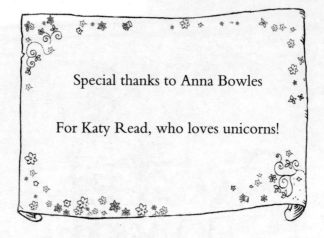

Special thanks to Anna Bowles

For Katy Read, who loves unicorns!

ORCHARD BOOKS
338 Euston Road, London NW1 3BH
Orchard Books Australia
Level 17/207 Kent Street, Sydney, NSW 2000
A Paperback Original

First published in 2012 by Orchard Books

A CIP catalogue record for this book is available
from the British Library.

ISBN 978 1 40832 365 6

3 5 7 9 10 8 6 4 2

Printed and bound by CPI Group (UK) Ltd, Croydon, CR0 4YY

The paper and board used in this paperback are natural recyclable
products made from wood grown in sustainable forests. The
manufacturing processes conform to the environmental regulations
of the country of origin.

Orchard Books is a division of Hachette Children's Books,
an Hachette UK company

www.hachette.co.uk

Series created by Hothouse Fiction
www.hothousefiction.com

Unicorn Valley

ROSIE BANKS

ORCHARD

Contents

A New Adventure

"There!" said Ellie Macdonald, standing back to admire the pretty shapes laid out on the baking tray.

It was a rainy Sunday afternoon and her best friends Summer Hammond and Jasmine Smith had come round to make biscuits. Summer had designed hers in the shape of hearts, while Jasmine had made crowns. Artistic Ellie had created biscuit fairies.

"How long do we cook them for?" asked Summer, twirling one of her blonde pigtails thoughtfully. "I don't want them to burn!"

"Fifteen minutes," said Ellie, consulting the cookbook.

"Fifteen minutes!" wailed Jasmine dramatically, slumping down in her chair so that her glossy black hair flew around her face. "But I'm starving!"

"It'll go by in a flash," Ellie giggled. "I'll get the timer."

She jumped up from the table where they had been working, then stumbled as she caught her foot on the leg of her chair.

"Oops," she said as it clattered to the floor.

Mrs Macdonald came in to see what

the noise was. "Don't you worry, girls,"
she said, admiring the biscuits. "I'll put
these in to bake, and call you when
they're done. I'm sure they'll be delicious.
And you've made such lovely shapes!
Crowns and hearts and even fairies. What
imaginations you all have."

While Mrs Macdonald was
putting the biscuits into the
oven, the three friends
exchanged a grin. Of
course Ellie's mum
thought they had
good imaginations
– she hadn't been to
the Secret Kingdom, the
magical land where only
a few days ago the girls had
actually met a real king wearing a real

crown, seen fairies, and eaten magical heart-shaped endless cookies at King Merry's birthday party!

"Let's go upstairs while the biscuits are baking," suggested Jasmine loudly. "And check on the Magic Box," she added quietly as the girls headed up to Ellie's room. "Just in case! You did bring it, didn't you, Summer?"

"Of course," Summer said with a smile.

Ellie's bedroom was long and light, with her art books and tools scattered across a big desk and the colourful pictures she'd painted pinned all over the lilac walls.

The girls settled down on the big window seat where Ellie did her painting. Summer carefully pulled the Magic Box out of her bag and passed it to Jasmine, who stared eagerly at its mirrored lid.

The box was just as beautiful as when they had first found it. Its wooden sides were delicately carved with images of magical creatures and its curved lid had a mirror surrounded by six glittering green stones.

"It was so lucky we found this at the school jumble sale," smiled Summer.

"We didn't find it – it found us!" Jasmine reminded her. "The Magic Box knew we were the only ones who could help the Secret Kingdom."

The Secret Kingdom was an amazing place where lots of magical creatures lived – but it had a big problem. Ever since its subjects had chosen King Merry to rule instead of Queen Malice, his nasty sister, Malice had been determined to make everyone in the kingdom as miserable as she was. She'd scattered six horrible thunderbolts around the land, and each of them contained a spell to cause lots of trouble.

"The kingdom still needs our help, though," said Ellie. "We stopped Queen Malice's first thunderbolt from wrecking King Merry's birthday party, but we've only found one of the thunderbolts she hid. Trixibelle said there were six."

"I hope we see Trixi again soon," said Summer. "It was so wonderful meeting a real pixie."

"Well it doesn't look like we'll be seeing her today," said Jasmine sadly, putting the Magic Box down and flopping onto Ellie's homemade rag rug. "The mirror's blank."

"No, it isn't!" exclaimed Ellie, grabbing the box and leaning over it. "Look!"

The mirror was starting to glimmer and shine. Words began to float up from its shimmering depths.

"It's a riddle!" said Ellie. She read the words in the mirror out loud:

"The second thunderbolt is found
Where one-horned creatures
walk the ground.
Its wicked magic must be foiled
Before a special game is spoiled!"

Ellie crinkled her forehead thoughtfully.

"Creatures with one horn," she said. "I don't know about you, but that makes me think of…"

"Unicorns!" broke in Summer, her eyes shining. "There were unicorns at King Merry's birthday party! But I don't know where they live."

At that moment, the Magic Box began to glow even brighter. Slowly it opened, and a fountain of light shot up from the centre, lifting up a square of parchment. It was the magical map King Merry had

given them after their last adventure!
Jasmine unfolded it carefully. It showed
the crescent moon-shaped island of the
Secret Kingdom. All three girls crowded
round.

"There's King Merry's palace," Jasmine said, pointing to the pink building with its four golden turrets. The flags at the top of the turrets waved slightly, as if in a breeze.

Summer was looking around the rest of the map. "Flower Forest," she read out. "Dolphin Bay."

"What's that?" asked Jasmine, pointing to a wooded area surrounded by steep hills.

Ellie looked closer. "Unicorn Valley!" she exclaimed. "That must be where the next thunderbolt is!"

They all looked at the Magic Box, but nothing happened.

"What did we do before?" Summer wondered aloud.

"We put our hands on the jewels, then Trixi and King Merry appeared!" Jasmine remembered. The Magic Box started to glow again, and the friends rushed to press their palms onto the brilliant jewels.

"The answer to the riddle is Unicorn Valley!" Ellie whispered.

For a moment the light coming from the box flashed so brightly they had to shut their eyes. Then it died away, and everything was still.

The girls looked around cautiously.

"Do you think it worked?" asked Jasmine. "King Merry and Trixi appeared in Summer's wardrobe last time."

All three of them looked towards Ellie's wardrobe. Then, behind them, the lid of Ellie's toy chest started to rattle. . .

Ellie saw it out of the corner of her eye and turned round so fast she almost fell over. "They're stuck in the toy chest!" she cried.

"Don't worry," came a tinkly little voice from among the toys. "I'll be with you in a moment."

"Trixi!" the girls cried happily, recognising the voice of King Merry's royal pixie, who had guided them around the Secret Kingdom during their last visit.

As they watched, pink petals began to creep around the edge of the lid of the chest. The flowers were growing magically fast, forcing it apart. The lid

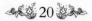

burst open with a shower of petals and
Trixi shot out, riding on a leaf. The tiny
pixie waved at the girls excitedly, then
tapped the magical ring she always
wore. It sparkled and the magic flowers
dissolved into glittery dust that settled on
Ellie's floor before gradually fading away.

Then Trixi floated over to where the
girls were standing. "It's lovely to see you
again," she smiled, flying her leaf over to
each of them in turn and kissing them on
the nose.

"You too," said Summer happily. After
their last adventure it had hardly seemed
real that they had made friends with a
pixie, but here she was, looking just the
same – her clothes made out of leaves,
messy blonde hair peeking out from
under her flower hat.

Trixi's blue eyes twinkled as she smiled at them all.

"But where's King Merry?" Jasmine asked.

"He's busy writing a speech," Trixi told her. "Every year the unicorns hold an event called the Golden Games and King Merry gives a welcome speech to everyone there. Except last time he got confused and arrived at the end of the games, so I had to turn it into a goodbye speech instead!"

The girls all giggled. It was so nice to hear about the Secret Kingdom. But it was even better to go there and have adventures themselves!

"Poor King Merry," laughed Jasmine.

"Well, he might be in trouble again this year," said Ellie seriously. "The riddle says that Queen Malice's second thunderbolt is hidden in Unicorn Valley."

"Oh, no!" exclaimed Trixi. "Let's see if we can spot it." She flew over the map and hovered over Unicorn Valley.

They looked down into an orchard full
of fruit trees, neat gardens, a steep hill
surrounded by multicoloured grass and
beautiful emerald-green fields.

"Unicorn Valley is one of the loveliest spots
in the kingdom," said Trixi. "Just the sort of
place Queen Malice would try to wreck!"

"Well, we won't let her," said Ellie
firmly.

"Let's go!" said Jasmine.

Trixi gave the Magic Box a tap with
her ring. Then she chanted:

"The evil Queen has trouble planned.
Brave helpers fly to save our land!"

Trixi's words appeared on the mirrored
lid before streaming up to the ceiling.
They swirled around in a dancing cloud

and then surrounded the girls' heads in a
glittering, flashing whirlwind.

"We're off to the Secret Kingdom!"
cried Jasmine above the sound of rushing
air.

The girls grabbed one another's hands
as Ellie's bedroom seemed to drop away
beneath them. There was a flash of
blinding colours…and there, spread out
below them just as they had been on the
map, but much more beautiful, were the
rolling green fields of Unicorn Valley.

Fields that were getting closer and
closer very quickly!

"Aaarrgh!" shrieked Ellie, screwing her
eyes shut. "We're falling!"

Into the Valley

"We're not falling, we're hang-gliding!"
called Jasmine from nearby.

Ellie realised that something was
wrapped around her body, holding her
safe. She looked up and saw a huge red
leaf, fluttering delicately in the wind
above her head. Vines descended from it,
looping safely around her waist.

"I think I can see the whole of Unicorn Valley," called Summer, who was drifting towards Ellie underneath a huge yellow leaf. In the centre of the valley was an enormous tree that towered over all the others.

"That's the Great Apple Tree," said Trixi, who was flying along beside them on her own magical leaf. "It was the first tree that ever grew in Unicorn Valley."

"Um, it's lovely," agreed Ellie, a bit nervously. "But how do we land?"

"There's a patch of moss just down there," said Trixi. She pointed to a corner of a field filled with flowers. "That will work as a nice soft landing pad. Careful now!"

Flapping their arms and giggling, the girls steered their leaves down to land on the bouncy blue moss. Their leaves settled on top of them with a soft *flump* sound.

"Phew!" said Ellie from under her leaf, which had covered her like a collapsed tent. She pulled it off, but it caught something on her head. Ellie put up her hand to free it and realised she was wearing the beautiful tiara King Merry had given her at the end of their last adventure! She grinned and scrambled about, calling, "Trixi! Are you there?"

"I certainly am," said the little pixie.

Ellie climbed out from under her leaf, and nearly fell over in shock at what she saw. Two white unicorns were galloping gracefully towards them.

Their manes flowed in the wind and their horns sparkled in the sunshine – one silver and one gold. Ellie turned to look in wonder at Summer and Jasmine. Their tiaras had appeared magically on their heads too, and they were both staring open-mouthed at the beautiful creatures.

The bigger unicorn had a beautiful wreath of plaited leaves and berries resting on her mane. When she reached the girls she stopped and gently touched the tip of her horn to each of their heads.

"That's a special sign of greeting," Trixi whispered to them. "You should curtsy."

Hastily, Summer and Ellie picked up the edges of their skirts and curtsied clumsily. Jasmine, who was wearing jeans, had to hold out the edges of her top.

"Welcome to Unicorn Valley," said the

unicorn in a regal voice. "I am Silvertail,
leader of the unicorns, and this is my
daughter, Littlehorn. You are the first
humans I have seen in a long time."

The smaller unicorn whinnied. "I've
never seen a human before," she said. She
trotted round the girls, looking at them
closely. "You haven't even got tails!" she
said in disbelief.

Ellie and Jasmine giggled, but Summer was too awestruck. "I can't believe we're talking to real, live unicorns!" she whispered to Ellie.

Trixi flew her leaf around to hover in front of the girls and cleared her throat. "Jasmine, Ellie and Summer are honoured guests of King Merry," she explained.

"We know," said Silvertail with a smile. She turned to face the girls. "We can tell from your tiaras that you are Very Important Friends of his. Everyone in the kingdom is talking about how you saved King Merry's birthday party from Queen Malice's nasty thunderbolt!" She shook her mane and harrumphed at the thought of the wicked queen.

"We think that another thunderbolt might have landed here in Unicorn

Valley," Ellie told her. "We have to find it before it causes any damage."

Silvertail whinnied anxiously. "My orchard-keepers did say that there was something strange near the Great Apple Tree. I was on my way there when you arrived. Perhaps you should come with me?"

"Of course we will," Jasmine agreed.

"It'll be faster if you ride," Silvertail said, looking sideways at the girls' legs. "I will summon my strongest unicorns to carry you."

The three girls exchanged excited glances.

"We're going to ride on unicorns?" cried Jasmine.

Silvertail turned towards the fields and tossed her head. At once, three sturdy

unicorns came galloping up. One was a
minty green, one was a deep midnight blue
and the last was a charcoal grey. All of
them had long, dark manes and tails, and
swirly, golden horns. Silvertail introduced
them as Fleetfoot, Sleekmane and Greycoat.

"We'll have a wonderful view from
up here," said Jasmine, climbing onto
Fleetfoot's mint-green back.

"But we're not too high!" said Ellie,
settling onto Greycoat. "Just how I like it!"

"Thank you for carrying us," said
Summer to Sleekmane. "This is the first
time I've been on a unicorn."

"Hold on tight!" replied Sleekmane with a
friendly whinny.

With Trixi hovering beside them, the
friends followed Silvertail across Unicorn
Valley.

"Have the unicorns always lived here?"
asked Ellie.

"No," Silvertail explained. "Unicorn
Valley was founded by a unicorn called
Snowmane thousands of years ago. Back
then, this whole area was covered with
poisonous prickles and carnivorous plants.
It was the wildest place in the whole
kingdom. But then Snowmane touched
a thorn bush with her horn and turned
it into a lovely magic apple tree. The tree
spread its beauty out across the land, and
all the awful plants disappeared."

Littlehorn swished her tail, cantering
between her mother and the unicorns
who carried the girls. "We look after
the orchards and keep Unicorn Valley a
magical place," she neighed happily.

"Those are the stables, where we sleep,"

said Silvertail, nodding towards a golden building that was set back from the road in a meadow full of flowers. "And up ahead you can see Happyhooves Academy, our school."

"Oh, the baby unicorns are *so* cute!" exclaimed Summer.

The group slowed down to admire the unicorn school, which was a big field divided into lots of open-air classrooms. Riding on their strong unicorn friends, Ellie, Jasmine and Summer were soon close enough to see a teacher showing some very young unicorns how to write their names. Concentrating hard, they moved their horns through the air and glittery, floating letters appeared in front of them.

"Those little unicorns have silver horns,

like you," said Summer to Littlehorn. "But all the big unicorns have gold horns."

"Our horns stay silver until we're grown up," explained Littlehorn. "Then we take part in the Golden Games and the elders turn our horns golden. You're here just at the right time – the games are this

afternoon! I'm competing in the Great
Race. The winner gets to be one of the
King's royal messengers and carry urgent
letters around the kingdom. It's a huge
honour!"

"I'm sure that's why the Magic Box
has called us now," Jasmine whispered in
Ellie's ear. "Queen Malice's thunderbolt is
going to wreck the Golden Games!"

"Not if we can help it!" Ellie replied
with a grin.

After a short trip, the girls trotted into
the orchards, where hundreds of neat trees
were being tended by older unicorns.

"This is the Royal Apple Orchard,"
Silvertail explained, "where all the apples
in the Secret Kingdom grow."

"Oh, I wish I had my art supplies so I
could draw it!" cried Ellie. "The orchard is

so lovely… Or I could draw the stable…
No, the baby unicorns!"

Silvertail smiled. "Come with me just
a little further," she said, "and I will
show you the prettiest sight in the whole
valley."

Fleetfoot, Sleekmane and Greycoat
cantered between two rows of neat trees
and came out in a clearing.

Right in the centre was the enormous
tree the girls had seen as they glided into
the kingdom. It was even bigger close up.

"Its trunk is as big as my house!" gasped
Jasmine.

The unicorns knelt so that Ellie,
Summer and Jasmine could jump down
and walk over to the tree. Its ancient
branches stretched out above them, heavy
with gleaming apples.

"This is the Great Apple Tree that Snowmane created," said Silvertail. "Without it, Unicorn Valley would turn back into a wild and dark place."

"It's amazing!" breathed Ellie.

"This is where the orchard-keepers said they saw something strange," said Silvertail. "Maybe the thunderbolt is hidden nearby."

The girls started looking all over the trunk of the tree. Trixi flew her leaf high up into the branches. But they couldn't see any sign of Queen Malice's thunderbolt.

Suddenly there was a whinny of alarm from the other side of the tree. Trixi gave the girls a worried glance, and they all ran round to see what was the matter.

Silvertail was there, staring at something stuck deep in the earth between the roots of the Great Apple Tree. It was a hard black shard that glistened horribly – the tip of Queen Malice's thunderbolt!

"Oh, no!" Silvertail neighed urgently.

"Queen Malice's nasty thunderbolt is in the roots of the Great Apple Tree! If the tree is hurt, its magic will disappear, and the whole valley will go back to being a wasteland!"

Slimy Caterpillars and Twisty Vines

The girls started inspecting the tree's lower branches to check for damage.

"I'll check the fruit," Littlehorn said. She concentrated hard and with a wave of her horn an apple floated down from the top of the tree. It landed on the ground in front of her. Littlehorn nudged it with her horn and then froze.

"What's wrong?" Summer asked. As she watched, a lump rose on the apple's rosy skin. Then it burst – and out came the head of a big, purple, black-spotted caterpillar.

"That's a slime caterpillar!" Trixi cried. "They usually live on the other side of the kingdom, in the grounds of Queen

Malice's horrible Thunder Castle. The more they eat, the bigger they get!"

The funny-looking creature nosed around in the warm air and stuck its tongue out at the girls before burrowing back out of sight.

"Yuck!" gasped Ellie, stepping backwards into Littlehorn, who stumbled and knocked over a basketful of apples.

The fruit spilled out onto the ground, and more caterpillars fell out with it.

"Ugh, they're horrible!" said Jasmine, looking at one of the slimy creatures, which was chomping on an apple enthusiastically.

Summer watched a caterpillar as it swallowed a big chunk of apple and then burped loudly. "They're just hungry," she said, kindly.

"Summer, you'd love any animal – no matter how disgusting it was!" Ellie teased her friend.

"Let's see if I can get rid of them," said Trixi, guiding her leaf down next to the nearest caterpillar and tapping it with her ring. She chanted:

"You greedy things aren't wanted here.
This spell will make you disappear!"

Nothing happened.

"Queen Malice's magic is too strong for me," Trixi sighed.

The girls exchanged dismayed looks.

"We'll have to destroy the thunderbolt,"
Silvertail said. "I'll get my strongest
unicorns and we'll pull it right out of the
ground."

"It's no use," Trixi told her. "In order to
get rid of the thunderbolt we'll have to
break Queen Malice's spell."

"What will we do if the caterpillars
hurt the tree?" Littlehorn asked. She was
standing beneath the Great Apple Tree,
gazing unhappily at the caterpillars,
who were wriggling
about among the
spilled apples
and chomping
happily.
A big,
sparkling
teardrop

rolled from one of her eyes. Where it splashed onto the grass, a tiny flower started to grow. "If the valley turns back the way it was, we'll have nowhere to go."

Silvertail looked at her daughter. "Why don't you go and practise for the race, Littlehorn?" she said kindly. "It'll take your mind off things. And you girls could all go and watch," she suggested, turning to Ellie, Summer and Jasmine. "Maybe you'll be able to find more clues about what Queen Malice is up to, and how to stop her. My orchard-keepers are the best gardeners in the Secret Kingdom. I'm sure they can take care of the caterpillars until we find out how to break Malice's spell. And I'll stay here to help them."

"And I'll put a holding spell around the tree so that the caterpillars can't spread to the rest of the orchard," Trixi told them.

"Yes, let's go to the practice," Summer said to Littlehorn comfortingly, stroking her hand along the unicorn's coat. "We'll probably come up with an idea there."

The little unicorn nodded bravely and led the way out of the out of the apple orchards, towards the racetrack. As they walked into the gardens, the girls looked around them anxiously, trying to spot any other signs of Queen Malice's mischief.

Summer noticed that Littlehorn was looking down at her hooves as she walked, with a worried expression on her face.

"Why don't you tell us about the Golden Games?" Summer asked to distract her.

The little unicorn looked happier at the thought of the afternoon's fun.

"Well, there's the Great Race, of course," she said. "And there are lots of other games and sports, and feats of unicorn magic too."

"That sounds brilliant," smiled Summer as the girls reached the racetrack. It circled a playing field and a small hill, which was already crowded with unicorns watching the others practise. The track was covered with grass that grew in coloured lines to show the runners where to go.

"What game are they playing?" asked Summer, pointing to some unicorns on the big field inside the track, who were leaping up at shining golden hoops that floated magically in the air and catching them on their horns.

"That's Unicorn-Horn Hoopla," said Littlehorn proudly. "And over there,

they're having a game of Run-Away
Rounders."

The girls watched a team of unicorns
who were using their horns to hit a
bright red ball. Every time the ball hit the
ground it sprouted little legs and tried to
run away from the fielders.

"Look, there's King Merry!" said Ellie,
pointing excitedly. The little king looked
very smart in his royal robes, except that
he had bits of paper sticking out of all his
pockets, and ink stains on his cloak.

He was pacing up and down beside the
track, scratching his head so hard that
his half-moon spectacles were knocked
almost off his nose.

"He looks worried," said Trixi. "I'd
better see if he's okay."

Summer, Ellie and Jasmine hurried over

to the king, who was muttering to himself absentmindedly.

"Now, let me see," he said. "It is your honour to address me today… Dearie me, no, that's not right. I mean, it is my honour to address you tomorrow… Oh my goodness, no, that won't do either."

"Is he practising his welcome speech?" Summer whispered to Trixi.

"I think he must be," replied the pixie. "He's not very good at remembering his lines!"

The king stopped pacing and patted his pockets as if he was looking for something. Trixi flew forward and conjured up a large spotted hanky, magicking his robes clean and tidy at the same time.

"Hello!" King Merry said cheerfully. "Girls, how nice to see you again. Are you here for the games?"

"Not quite," Ellie explained. "The Magic Box has brought us here. There's a thunderbolt in the roots of the Great Apple Tree."

"And it's already causing trouble," said Jasmine. "There are horrible slime caterpillars attacking the tree."

"How terrible!" said the king. "Do you have a plan to get rid of the thunderbolt?" He looked at the girls hopefully.

"Not yet," Ellie admitted. "But we're working on it."

"Wow, look at her go!" Summer said, pointing at Littlehorn, who was now racing around the coloured track with five other young unicorns. "She's so fast!"

In spite of her worries, Summer couldn't help smiling as the beautiful creatures galloped along, urging one another on. "We won't let the unicorns down," she promised King Merry.

But just as the words left her mouth, something dreadful happened!

Right in front of the racing unicorns, a cluster of long green weeds broke

through the surface of the track. The
thick stalks immediately began to
grow, snaking out across the grass in all
directions. The nasty
plants slithered out
and tangled
themselves in
the legs of
the running
unicorns.
Four of the
runners got so
tripped up they
fell horn over hoof.
Littlehorn only escaped by
leaping high into the air as a stalk tried
to grab her tail.

"What on earth are those?" cried Ellie
as one of the weeds burst up through

the ground at Jasmine's feet. Ellie and
Summer grabbed it and pulled as hard as
they could, but the wriggling stem slipped
out of their hands and kept on growing.

"It must be because of the Great Apple
Tree!" Trixi cried. "With the caterpillars
eating the fruit, the tree must be getting
weaker. And with its magic fading, the
horrible weeds are coming back to
Unicorn Valley! Quick, head for the hill!"

Everyone started running up the hill,
but new vines began springing up all
around them, and they had to dodge the
stalks as they ran. The girls and unicorns
managed to scramble to the top of the
hill quickly, but King Merry lagged
behind. He was out of breath, and Trixi
had to help push him up the slope. They
had almost reached the girls when a

weed curled around King Merry's foot
and tripped him up.

Ellie dashed down to help him, but one
of the vines wound around her waist. As
Summer and Jasmine watched in horror,
the vicious vine started pulling her down
the hill!

Storm Sprites!

"Get off my friend!" Jasmine shouted, hitting the stalk that was wound tightly around Ellie.

"Hold on!" Summer called, grabbing Ellie's hands.

Jasmine started tugging at the clinging vine. With both of them working together, the weed's grip soon started to loosen.

"It's working!" exclaimed Ellie. The vine finally lost its grip – and she, Jasmine and Summer fell over in a big heap on the ground.

"Phew!" Ellie breathed. "That was close!" The girls struggled back to the top of the hill, where Trixi, King Merry, Littlehorn and the other unicorns were standing.

"The weeds are growing out of control!" exclaimed Jasmine, pointing down the hill, where even more yucky plants were popping up.

"We'll have to cancel the Golden Games," frowned King Merry. "There's no way we can hold them here with all these weeds in the way. Trixi, could you send a glow-worm announcement to warn everyone to stay away?"

Trixi tapped her ring, and it began to shine softly. A few moments later lots of little lights appeared around them as hundreds of glow-worms woke up. The girls looked in amazement at the little lights that shone weakly in the daylight.

"There are glow-worms right across the kingdom," Trixi explained. "They'll pass our message on to everyone who sees them."

Trixi flew over to tell the glow-worms the message, but Summer stopped her.

"Oh, please don't call off the games yet," she begged. "If you do, Queen Malice will get her way and all the unicorns will be miserable. Littlehorn and the others won't be able to get their golden horns, and King Merry won't get a new messenger. We have to fix this!"

"But what can we do?" Trixi cried anxiously. "Without the Great Apple Tree's magic, the valley will soon be completely ruined."

"Wait a minute," Ellie said. "We need to work out how we're going to break Queen Malice's thunderbolt. At King Merry's birthday party, we broke the spell by making sure everyone had fun. So if Queen Malice wants to ruin the Golden Games and the Great Race, then we have to make sure that they go ahead."

"But how?" Silvertail said. "We'll never clear all these weeds away in time, and we can't have the Great Race without a racetrack."

Summer smiled. "I have an idea! There's always a balance in nature, even if Queen Malice's magic is involved. We've got hungry caterpillars at the Great Apple Tree, and plants that won't stop growing at the racetrack...I think we should take the caterpillars to the Golden Games!"

"The caterpillars won't enjoy the games!" King Merry spluttered. "They're very lazy and they don't like sports."

Ellie smiled as she realised what her friend had in mind. "Not to take part in the games!" she laughed. "If we bring the greedy caterpillars here, they'll eat up all the weeds!"

"They'll chomp the racetrack clean!" agreed Jasmine.

"And then the games can go on!" Summer said, beaming.

Trixi danced excitedly around on her leaf. "I really think it might work, girls," she said. "Thank goodness you're here!"

"But how are we going to get back to the Great Apple Tree?" Jasmine asked, looking down at the weeds that were snaking all over the racetrack. "We're stranded!"

"I can take care of that!" Trixi said cheerfully. "Everyone hold hands – or hooves."

"I'll stay here, Trixi," King Merry announced. "Someone has to stay with the other unicorns and keep them calm."

"He doesn't like being magicked around," Trixi whispered to the girls. "It tangles up his beard and makes him dizzy!"

The girls giggled.

With Ellie, Summer, Jasmine and Littlehorn all holding on to one another, Trixi cast a spell:

"Help us get where we need to be
Under the Great Apple Tree!"

Ellie shut her eyes tightly, and when she opened them again they were all standing in the clearing by the tree. She hadn't felt a thing!

"The caterpillars are much bigger now," Summer said.

Trixi's magic spell was keeping the slime caterpillars from spreading, but they were growing quickly as they munched apple after apple and nibbled on the tree trunk.

One of the orchard-keeper unicorns sighed. "And the larger they get, the more they eat!"

"That's a good thing!" grinned Jasmine. "There are lots of horrible weeds growing at the racetrack, and the caterpillars can help us by eating them all up! We just need to get them there…" Just then, she spotted a large apple cart nearby, with just a few fruits in it. "Aha!" she said. "That'll be perfect! If we load that cart full of the tastiest apples, the caterpillars are sure to jump in there too."

Trixi released her holding spell and Ellie and Summer set to work heaping armfuls of fruit into the cart. But the caterpillars paid no attention.

"If only we could get them to understand where we want them to go," said Summer, thoughtfully.

"How could we do that?" asked Trixi.

Summer thought for a moment longer. "We need a trail of food to lead the caterpillars all the way to the cart."

"That's an excellent idea!" said Trixi,

smiling. "I'll do it right away."

The little pixie tapped her ring. It glowed, then something green unfurled from it and fell to the ground. It was a crisp, fresh cabbage leaf.

More leaves appeared from her ring, and Trixi arranged them in a line, leading from the Great Apple Tree into the cart.

One of the caterpillars raised its head, sniffing the air. Then it licked its lips hungrily, crawled forward and began to nibble at the leaf.

It wasn't long before excited caterpillars were following one another towards the cart. One by one they oozed closer and crawled up into the cart, leaving a slimy trail behind them.

Once all the caterpillars were gathered up, the girls packed more apples and

berries around them to make sure they
had plenty to eat.

When everyone was ready, Trixi tapped
her ring once more and the whole group
was instantly transported back to the hill.

It was worse than they'd imagined. The
racetrack was completely covered with
horrible weeds, and King Merry was
marooned at the top of the hill next to
two sad-looking unicorns.

"We've brought the caterpillars from the Great Apple Tree," Ellie called up to him from the other side of the track. "They'll soon gobble up these vines!"

By now, the caterpillars had finished eating the food in the cart. When the girls looked in, there was nothing to be seen except apple cores and enormous, sleepy caterpillars.

"What if they're too full to eat the weeds?" Summer asked anxiously.

But when the slimy creatures spotted the moving weeds, they woke up at once. They licked their lips and crawled towards them eagerly, making funny little gobbling sounds. They quickly began to chomp their way through the mass of twisty green stalks.

"Our plan is working!" Trixi said, clapping her hands delightedly and flying her leaf in a figure of eight.

"Good job, Ellie, Summer and Jasmine!" King Merry called, leading the unicorns down the hill.

"Soon the racetrack will be clear!" said Jasmine as the girls moved the rest of the caterpillars off the carts. "Nothing's going to stop us now!"

Ellie gasped and grabbed her friend's arm. "Uh oh, something might," she said, pointing behind them. "Look back there."

The girls turned to look. Not far away, two horrid-looking creatures were flying towards the racetrack on top of thunderclouds. Their spiky fingers were outstretched and their dark eyes gleamed with nastiness.

"Queen Malice's Storm Sprites!" said
Summer.

The ugly creatures zoomed closer on
their thunderclouds. One of them blew
a raspberry at the girls.

"Give those caterpillars
to us!" the other
one shouted.
"We're going
to spread them
everywhere so
they eat every
single plant, tree
and bush around.
Unicorn Valley will
become a wasteland, and there's nothing
you can do!"

A Slimy Surprise

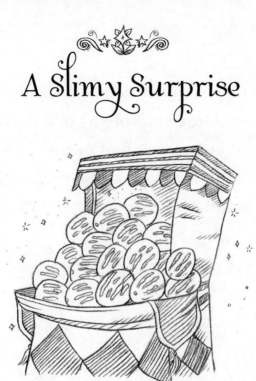

"We can't let the Storm Sprites take the caterpillars!" Summer cried.

Just then, Jasmine noticed something by the entrance to the racetrack – a stand full of juicy-looking blue melons.

"Quick, help me grab some really big caterpillars," Jasmine said. "No time to explain – just trust me."

Ellie and Summer helped Jasmine
find three large caterpillars and carry
them towards the stall of melons. The
caterpillars were so fat now that each girl
could only lift one of them, and they were
very slimy!

"Phew!" puffed Ellie as she put her heavy caterpillar in place. "I get it, Jasmine. The caterpillars will make the ground slippery, and the Storm Sprites will fall over!"

"Brilliant idea," Trixi said as she flew overhead. "Those are sugar-melons. They're so sweet and tasty the caterpillars won't be able to resist them!"

Sure enough, as soon as the caterpillars spotted the yummy-looking sugar-melons, they crawled eagerly across the path to get to them, leaving three super-slippery trails behind them.

"Okay, you win," Jasmine called to the sprites. "We'll give you the caterpillars. Here, take these ones."

The sprites laughed nastily, then hopped off their thunderclouds and flew down to the ground, narrowing their black eyes as if they were getting ready to spring.

"Whoa!" shouted the first sprite as he landed. "It's slippery!"

His foot shot out from underneath him and hit the other sprite on the ankle. The second sprite gave a wail, hopped on one leg, then stumbled his way across the road, waving his arms frantically.

The Storm Sprites had landed right in the slippery caterpillar goo!

Neither of them could find a firm place to stand. First they slid into each other, then they tried to grab each other. Finally they both fell down in a tangled heap among the sugar-melons.

"You knocked me over, Slug-Breath," one of them shouted.

"No, you tripped me up!" the other complained bitterly from underneath a squashed melon.

The girls stood beside the road, giggling at the sight of Queen Malice's henchmen lying surrounded by squashed melons and slime.

The unicorns laughed too – all except Fleetfoot, Greycoat and Sleekmane, who were standing over the Storm Sprites, giving them very stern looks.

"You two are coming with us," Greycoat whinnied. "You can help us tidy up the orchard. That should keep you out of trouble until the Golden Games are over."

The unicorns marched the Storm Sprites off towards the orchard, with the sprites still bickering loudly and pushing and shoving each other.

"There won't *be* any games unless the caterpillars have cleared the track," Jasmine said anxiously. But when she looked at the racecourse, there wasn't a weed to be seen! The grass was visible again, and lying sleepily on it, looking fatter than ever, were the slime caterpillars! The one closest to Jasmine was lying on his back, with his hundreds of feet up in the air, snoring loudly.

Suddenly there was a whinny, and
Silvertail came racing up to them
from the direction of the Great Apple
Tree. "Queen Malice's thunderbolt has
broken!" she told them excitedly. "The

tree has already begun to repair itself!"

"We did it!" cried Jasmine.

"We will always be grateful for what you have done today," Silvertail said gravely. "But I am afraid there is still one problem."

The friends exchanged a look.

"The caterpillars!" they all said at once.

What were they going to do with the greedy creatures?

"We have to find somewhere else for them to live," said Trixi.

"Yes," Summer agreed. "We can't send the poor things back to Queen Malice."

But as they watched, the caterpillars started to wriggle. After a few moments, they had coated themselves in silk, which quickly hardened into a solid cocoon.

"What's happening?" King Merry

asked. Silvertail knelt down and nudged
the nearest cocoon with her horn.

"I don't know," she said, "but at least
they won't need feeding for a while!"
Everyone helped move the cocoons
carefully into the cart, where they'd be

out of the way of the Golden Games. It was a lot easier now that the caterpillars weren't wiggling around!

"Just in time!" said Silvertail, smiling as Jasmine put the last cocoon carefully into the cart. "We're ready for the Opening Ceremony. Summer, Ellie and Jasmine, you must stay and be our guests of honour."

Silvertail led the girls to the best spot on the hill, next to King Merry. Trixi magicked up floating cushions for them all, and they settled down as the young unicorns made the final preparations for the games.

Once everything was ready, King Merry's cushion floated up above the spectators and he nervously read out his speech.

"It is my address to honour you this year…" he started to say, getting his words hopelessly jumbled up again.

Summer, Ellie and Jasmine found it difficult not to giggle, but they didn't want to upset the kindly king. They did their best and managed to stay straight-faced until he had finished.

Then they forgot about laughing as the parade of competitors began. Lots of little unicorns strutted smartly around the track. They all had different ribbons, flowers and grasses woven into their manes and tails.

The girls all cheered as Littlehorn cantered past proudly.

Finally the unicorns lined up in front of the audience and sang the Secret Kingdom's national song:

"The Secret Kingdom is a
wonderful land
From frosty mountain to
glittery sand
Every unicorn, imp and gnome
Loves our beautiful magical home."

After they'd sung all the verses, the
stadium went quiet.

"Look!" Ellie cried,
pointing at the sky.
All the little
unicorns had
raised their heads,
and pink and
red sparkles were
shooting from the
tips of their horns

like fireworks! The sparkles swirled and twisted into huge letters that twinkled brightly in the evening sky.

"Thank you Summer,
Ellie and Jasmine
for breaking Queen
Malice's Spell!"

Summer read out loud.

"Wow!" breathed Jasmine.

Then the letters joined and changed, coming together again to spell out:

Let the Golden
Games begin!

The Golden Games

The girls oohed and aahed in wonder
as they saw one amazing event after
another. Some of the graceful unicorns
took part in a jumping race, leaping
over hurdles made of shimmering magic.
Others jumped high in the air to catch
golden hoops on their horns. There was
so much going on that Ellie, Summer and
Jasmine hardly knew where to look first!

The high point of the games was the Great Race. Summer, Ellie and Jasmine held on to their cushions with excitement as Silvertail fired a burst of sparkles from her horn to start the race and the unicorns sped off.

"Come on, Littlehorn!" chanted the girls.

At first Littlehorn was in the lead! But a larger, red-dappled unicorn was running on the inside lane, and he was gradually overtaking her…

Jasmine stood up and shouted encouragement while Ellie cheered and Summer crossed her fingers and pressed them against her cheeks.

Trixi was so excited she couldn't bear to look, so she hid behind her human friends. "Tell me when it's over!" she said.

Littlehorn put on a burst of speed, creeping closer and closer to the larger unicorn.

"You can do it, Littlehorn!" Jasmine yelled at the top of her voice. Littlehorn lowered her horn determinedly and galloped as fast as she could. She drew level with the other unicorn – and won by a head!

Trixi and the girls watched with pride as King Merry crowned Littlehorn with a wreath of glitterberries and officially named her as his new royal messenger.

Finally, all the young unicorns climbed up to the top of the hill and were greeted by their family and friends. The celebrations were nearly over and the girls knew it was almost time for them to go home. Only one last thing remained – to watch Littlehorn and the other young unicorns get their golden horns!

Silvertail whinnied and the unicorns all fell silent. "This is when we perform the coming-of-age ceremony," she said, "and where we honour those who help us."

Littlehorn suddenly looked very serious. She and the other young unicorns gathered in a circle facing inwards and slowly lowered their heads. As their horns touched, there was a tinkling sound, and the air above the circle started to glow. The girls gasped in wonder as the little unicorns' horns slowly changed from a sparkling silver to a glorious golden colour. As soon as the change was complete there was a great roar of noise as all the unicorns neighed and stomped their hooves in celebration. Littlehorn grinned widely, going cross-eyed in her attempts to look at her newly golden horn.

The noise died down as Silvertail moved into the middle of the circle. She gave a long whinny, and all of the unicorns pointed their horns to one spot in the air. Bursts of sparkly magic streamed out of their horns, coming together to form a glittery shape. Slowly the shape came into focus – it was a tiny silver unicorn horn! When it was complete, Silvertail whinnied again and the horn floated over to the girls.

"This is a gift to thank you for saving Unicorn Valley from Queen Malice's

meanness. Without you our beautiful
home would have been destroyed. We will
always be grateful," said Silvertail, bowing
to the girls. Behind her, the unicorns
bowed their heads. Even Trixi, with a
huge smile on her little face, dipped a
little curtsy.

Summer realised all the unicorns were
waiting for them to take the gift. She
stepped forward nervously and carefully
grasped the sparkling horn. It was no
longer than her little finger, and seemed
to weigh almost nothing.
It was covered with
a beautiful spiral
pattern, just like
Littlehorn's.
Just then
there was a
gasp from the
crowd. The
girls turned
and peered
down at the apple
carts. The caterpillar
cocoons were moving and

shaking. All of a sudden one of them popped open and a gorgeous butterfly with shimmering purple patterns on its wings flew up into the air! The cocoons were hatching! Soon another butterfly appeared, and then another, until the air was filled with them, dancing and fluttering about on their new wings.

"They're beautiful!" Summer exclaimed.

"Who'd have thought those slimy caterpillars could become such gorgeous butterflies," Jasmine smiled.

"I hope they won't be quite as hungry now they're grown up," Ellie worried.

Everyone admired the beautiful butterflies as they flitted and fluttered above, oohing and aahing at their dance in the sky.

After a few minutes, Silvertail hushed the crowd. "We will be silent for a moment," she said seriously. "Now, Summer, listen carefully.

Summer did so, wondering what was supposed to happen.

Then she gasped. Amongst the flapping of their wings she could suddenly hear the butterflies calling out.

"Thank you!" they all cried. "We didn't mean to cause any trouble."

"I can understand the butterflies!" she said in amazement.

Ellie and Jasmine listened hard. "I can't hear anything," Ellie said.

"The silver horn gives you the ability
to talk to and understand animals," said
Trixi, smiling.

Summer handed the horn to her friends
so that they could hear the little voices.

Trixi tapped her ring and a sparkly
spell in the shape
of a butterfly
appeared and
flew away,
leaving
a glittery
trail. "This
will lead
you to Flower
Forest," she told the
beautiful butterflies.

As the butterflies started
to follow Trixi's spell to their new home,

Silvertail turned to the girls solemnly. "You are now honorary members of our unicorn family. You are Summer Kindhoof, you are Ellie Flamemane and you are Jasmine Braveheart," she said as she gently touched each of the girls in turn with her horn. "Should you ever need us, we will be there to help you."

The girls looked at one another in amazement. "Thank you," Jasmine managed to say.

Smiling happily, the girls said goodbye to the unicorns. Trixi kissed each of them on the nose, then hovered above their heads and conjured up the magic whirlwind that would take them back home.

"See you soon!" was the last thing they heard as they were lifted higher and higher above beautiful Unicorn Valley.

Then, with a flash of light, they found themselves settling softly onto Ellie's rug.

Ordinary daylight filled the bedroom, and glinted off the Magic Box, which was sitting on the rug between them.

"Oh, wow," said Ellie, looking down at the little horn in her hand. "What an amazing adventure."

"I'm so glad we met the unicorns," said Summer.

"But it's a shame that time doesn't pass while we're in the Secret Kingdom," sighed Jasmine. "After all that, I'm hungrier than ever – and the biscuits *still* aren't ready!"

Ellie and Summer laughed.

Suddenly the Magic Box began to glow, and its lid slowly opened. Ellie gently placed the silver horn into one of the compartments inside. "I hope we can go back to the Secret Kingdom soon," she said.

"You can count on that, Flamemane," said Jasmine with a chuckle. "We still have to find four more of those nasty thunderbolts. I wonder where we'll go next. How about the Wandering

Waterfalls? Ooh, or the Mystic Meadows? King Merry said the pixies have toadstool fights there!"

"I'd love to see both of those places," sighed Summer. "But the important thing is to be there for Trixi and King Merry, and to save the kingdom from Queen Malice!"

"That's for certain," agreed Jasmine, grinning. "Right, then – race you to the biscuits!"

Laughing, the three friends ran downstairs.

In the next Secret Kingdom adventure, Ellie, Summer and Jasmine visit

Cloud Island!

Read on for a sneak peek...

A Message from the Secret Kingdom

"I wish we didn't have so much homework to do," sighed Ellie Macdonald as she walked home from school with her friends. "I've got to write a story for English and I don't know where to start!"

"Let's all do our homework together at my house," suggested Jasmine. "We can put some music on and help one another."

"Great idea," agreed Summer, linking arms with Jasmine and Ellie. "Even homework can be fun when you do it with friends."

"I wouldn't go that far," grinned Ellie, her green eyes twinkling. "But it's better than doing it on your own."

Laughing, they all made their way to Jasmine's house and piled into the kitchen.

A big packet of chocolate cookies and a note were sitting on the kitchen table. Jasmine picked up the note and read it out loud:

"Hi Jasmine, I'm sure you'll have brought Ellie and Summer back with you, so share these with them! There's some homemade lemonade in the fridge as well. See you at five. Mum."

"Your mum's so nice!" said Summer.

Jasmine smiled. "I wonder what made her think you'd be with me?"

"Yeah, anyone would think we spent all our time together," joked Ellie.

Summer giggled. She, Jasmine and Ellie all lived in a little village called Honeyvale, and went to the same school. They had been best friends since they were little, and they went around to one another's houses so much that they all felt like home!

Jasmine opened the fridge and took out a big jug of lemonade while Summer fetched three glasses and a plate.

"Now, let's get on with our homework," said Jasmine, putting everything on a tray and leading the way upstairs. "Then we can start having some real fun."

"Hey, you've got the Magic Box on your dressing table!" exclaimed Ellie as they all spilled into Jasmine's bedroom, which was quite small, but beautifully decorated. The walls were a gorgeous hot-pink colour, and red floaty netting hung down over the bed.

"I didn't want to miss a message from the Secret Kingdom!" Jasmine said.

They all looked at the beautiful wooden box. It was covered with intricate carvings of fairies and unicorns and had a mirrored lid studded with green stones. It looked like a jewellery box, but it was much more than that.

"I slept with it under my pillow last time I was looking after it!" Ellie laughed.

The girls had found the Magic Box at a school jumble sale, when it had mysteriously appeared in front of them. It belonged to King Merry, the ruler of the Secret Kingdom.

The Secret Kingdom was a magical world that no one knew existed – no one except Jasmine, Summer and Ellie! It was a beautiful crescent moon-shaped island, where mermaids, unicorns, pixies and elves all lived happily together.

But the kingdom was in terrible trouble. Queen Malice, the king's horrible sister, was so angry that the people of the Secret Kingdom had chosen King Merry to be their leader instead of her that she had sent six horrible thunderbolts into the kingdom to cause all kinds of trouble. Summer, Jasmine and Ellie had already found two of the thunderbolts and broken their nasty spells.

"I wish we could go on another magical adventure now," sighed Ellie.

"Me too," agreed Jasmine, taking her books out of her rucksack and sprawling out on the carpet. She tucked her long dark hair behind her ears. "Come on, let's get this over with," she said, reaching for a chocolate cookie.

Ellie got her English book out and started chewing on her pencil. She was looking round the room, trying to come up with an idea for her story, when something caught her eye. "I don't think we'll be doing homework after all!" she cried in delight. "The Magic Box is glowing!"

The girls all jumped up to look. They crowded around the box, watching excitedly as, letter by letter, words started to form in the magic mirror.

"I wonder what mischief Queen Malice is up to now," said Jasmine, shuddering at the thought of the horrid queen and her wicked plans to make everyone in the kingdom as miserable as she was.

"We'll have to solve the riddle to find out," said Summer, as she studied the words in the mirror. Then she slowly read them out loud:

"A thunderbolt there will be found
Way up high above the ground.
A white and fluffy floating land
Needs you all to lend a hand!"

Jasmine quickly wrote the riddle down before the words disappeared into the mirror. "What does it mean?" she asked.

Ellie looked puzzled. "A floating land – it must be an island."

"Let's check the map," said Jasmine. "We might be able to spot it."

As if it had heard them, the Magic Box opened up, revealing the six compartments inside. Only two of the spaces were filled, one by a map of the Secret Kingdom that King Merry had given them after their first visit, and the other by a little silver unicorn horn. It was small, but it had enormous power – whoever held it could talk to animals!

Summer carefully took out the map and gently spread it out on Jasmine's floor. The three girls sat round it, their heads touching as they peered at it excitedly. There were a few small islands in Mermaid Reef, and a couple more off the shore of Glitter Beach. They all moved magically on the map as the aquamarine sea bobbed up and down, but none of them looked white or fluffy.

"It's not here!" Summer said anxiously.

"But it has to be!" cried Ellie. "We have to solve the riddle so we can get to the Secret Kingdom and find the thunderbolt before something horrible happens!"

Jasmine stood up and started pacing up and down the middle of her room with a worried expression on her face.

"Let's read the riddle again," Summer suggested. "We have to be missing something. 'A white and fluffy floating land.' Well, these islands aren't white or fluffy."

"'Way up high above the ground…'" Jasmine muttered to herself. Then she glanced down at the map and laughed. Summer and Ellie were still searching the bottom of the map, looking at every inch of sea. But Jasmine had realised something. "We shouldn't be looking in the sea!" she cried. "We should be looking in the sky!"

"Of course!" said Ellie with a grin. "What's white and fluffy and floats?"

"A cloud!" exclaimed Summer.

"And here's Cloud Island!" Ellie exclaimed, pointing to a puffy white cloud at the top of the map. "That must be it. Let's summon Trixi!"

The girls put their hands on the Magic Box, pressing their fingers against the green stones on its carved wooden lid.

"The answer is Cloud Island," Jasmine whispered.

Suddenly there was a flash of light, followed by a squeal. Trixibelle had appeared, but the little pixie was trapped amongst the netting over Jasmine's bed!

"Keep still!" Jasmine cried as the little pixie twisted round. She was trying to free herself, but only succeeded in getting more and more caught up.

"I'm trying!" Trixi cried, giving a yelp as she tumbled off her leaf.

Ellie, Jasmine and Summer quickly climbed up onto Jasmine's bed to untangle Trixi from the gauze. Ellie's nimble fingers carefully unwrapped the netting from Trixi's flower hat, while Jasmine and Summer helped Trixi pull her arms and legs free.

"There!" Ellie said as she untangled the last bit.

"Phew!" Trixi sighed, jumping back on her leaf and flying in a quick twirl before straightening out her skirt and the flower hat that covered her messy blonde hair. "Hello, girls," she exclaimed, flying over to kiss them all on the tips of their noses. She landed on the edge of Jasmine's bedside table. "It's lovely to see you all again. Have you worked out where the next thunderbolt is?"

"We think it's somewhere called Cloud Island," Summer said.

Trixi nodded. "There's no time to waste! We need to go to the kingdom right away."

The girls all looked excitedly at one another. They were off on another magical adventure – this time to an island in the sky!

As the girls watched, Trixi tapped the
Magic Box with her ring and chanted a
spell:

"The evil Queen has trouble planned.
Brave helpers fly to save our land."

Her words appeared on the mirrored
lid and then soared towards the ceiling,
separated into sparkles and tumbled
down again in a colourful burst, whizzing
around the girls' heads until they formed
a whirlwind. The rushing air picked
the girls up, and moments later Ellie,
Summer and Jasmine were dropped onto
something springy. It was the softest
landing ever!

Summer looked round in astonishment.
It felt like she was on a huge bouncy

bed, but all she could see around her was white. Hesitantly she put out her hand to touch the fluffy stuff, and then grinned as she realised – she was standing on a cloud!

Read

Cloud Island

to find out what
happens next!

Be in on the secret.
Collect them all!

Enjoy six sparkling adventures.

Out now!

Secret Kingdom

A magical world of friendship and fun!

Join best friends
Ellie, Summer and Jasmine at

www.secretkingdombooks.com

and enjoy games, sneak peeks
and lots more!

You'll find great activities, competitions, stories
and games, plus a special newsletter for
Secret Kingdom friends!

Character Profile:
Summer Hammond

Personality:

Quiet, thoughtful and caring. If someone's upset, Summer will be the one to notice and help them.

Favourite Colour:

Yellow.

Loves:

Animals and reading.

Favourite Place in the Secret Kingdom:

Unicorn Valley. The baby unicorns are so cute!

Family:

Summer has one older brother, Phoenix, and two younger brothers, Finn and Connor. They all live with their mother and stepfather.

Caterpillar Maze

Jasmine, Ellie and Summer need to get the slime
caterpillars to the racetrack. Can you help
them find their way through the maze?
Watch out for Storm Sprites!

Secret Kingdom Codebreaker

Sssh! Can you keep a secret? Ellie, Summer and Jasmine have written a special message just for you! They have written one secret word of their special message in each of the six Secret Kingdom books.

To discover the secret word, hold a small mirror to this page and see your word magically appear!

The first secret word is: _____

When you have cracked the code and found all six secret words, work out the special message and go online to enter the competition at

www.secretkingdombooks.com

We will put all of the correct entries into a draw and select one winner to receive a special Secret Kingdom goody bag featuring lots of sparkly gifts, including a glittery t-shirt!

You can also send your entry on a postcard to:

Secret Kingdom Competition, Orchard Books, 338 Euston Road, London, NW1 3BH

Don't forget to include your name and address.

Good luck!

Closing Date: 31st October 2012.

Collect the tokens from each Secret Kingdom book to get special Secret Kingdom gifts!

In every Secret Kingdom book there are three Friendship Tokens that you can exchange for special gifts! Send your friendship tokens in to us as soon as you get them or save them up to get an even more special gift!

3 tokens

5 tokens

7 tokens

13 tokens

15 tokens

Secret Kingdom poster and collectable glittery bookmark

Pencil and rubber set

Pocket mirror

Two best friends friendship bracelets (one for you and one for your best friend)

Glittery t-shirt

To take part in this offer, please send us a letter telling us why you like Secret Kingdom. Don't forget to:
1) Tell us which gift you would like to exchange your tokens for
2) Include the correct number of Friendship Tokens for each gift you are requesting
3) Include your name and address
4) Include the signature of a parent or guardian

Secret Kingdom Friendship Token Offer
Orchard Books Marketing Department
338 Euston Road, London, NW1 3BH

Closing date: 31st October 2012

Terms and Conditions

(1) Open to UK and Republic of Ireland residents only (2) Purchase of the Secret Kingdom books is necessary (3) Please get the signature of your parent/guardian to enter this offer (4) The correct number of tokens must be included for the offer to be redeemed (5) Photocopied tokens will not be accepted (6) Prizes are distributed on a first come, first served basis whilst stocks last (7) No part of the offer is exchangeable for cash or any other offer (8) Please allow 28 days for delivery (9) We will use your data only for the purpose of fulfilling this offer (10) Prizes may vary from pictures shown. We reserve the right to offer prizes of an alternative or greater value.

www.secretkingdombooks.com

1 Friendship Token
www.secretkingdombooks.com

1 Friendship Token
www.secretkingdombooks.com

1 Friendship Token
www.secretkingdombooks.com

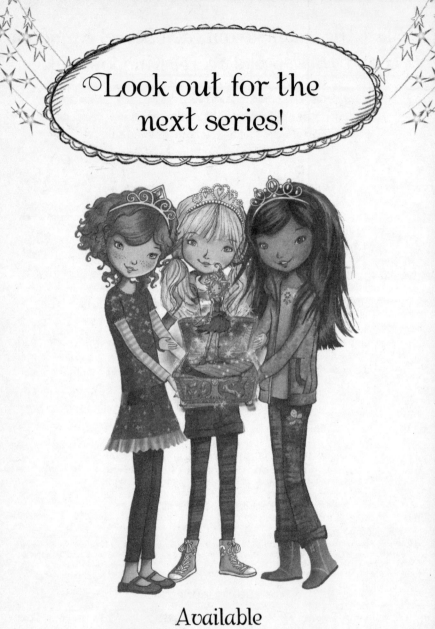

Look out for the next series!

Available
February 2013